D0328797

The GUMAZING GUM GIRL!

COVER BLOWN

RHODE MONTIJO

with Luke Reynolds

BOOK 4

DISNEP • HYPERION

LOS ANGELES   NEW YORK

Text and illustrations copyright © 2019 by Rhode Montijo

All rights reserved. Published by Disney • Hyperion, an imprint of Disney Book Group. No part of this book may be reproduced or transmitted in any form or by any means, electronic or mechanical, including photocopying, recording, or by any information storage and retrieval system, without written permission from the publisher. For information address Disney • Hyperion, 125 West End Avenue, New York, New York 10023.

First Edition, October 2019
1 3 5 7 9 10 8 6 4 2
FAC-038091-19228
Printed in the United States of America

This book is set in 14-pt. Grilled Cheese BTN Condensed/Fontbros

Designed by Phil Buchanan

Coloring by Joe To

Library of Congress Cataloging-in-Publication Data

Names: Montijo, Rhode, author, illustrator. • Reynolds, Luke, author.
Title: Cover blown / Rhode Montijo ; with Luke Reynolds.
Description: First edition. • Los Angeles ; New York : Disney Hyperion, 2019.
    • Series: The gumazing Gum Girl! ; [book 4] • Summary: When Gabby and her
    family visit her uncle in Cobá, México, she learns about her roots,
    and faces students from the wrestling school of her uncle's rival.
Identifiers: LCCN 2019009608 • ISBN 9781368048170 (hardcover)
Subjects: • CYAC: Superheroes—Fiction. • Hispanic Americans—Fiction. •
    Aztecs—Fiction. • Wrestling—Fiction. • Bubble gum—Fiction. •
    Mexico—Fiction.
Classification: LCC PZ7.M76885 Cov 2019 • DDC [Fic]—dc23
LC record available at https:// lccn.loc.gov/2019009608

Reinforced Binding

Visit www.DisneyBooks.com

For my wonderful wife, Sylvia, who helped me brainstorm the plot of this book while waiting in a four-hour line at Walt Disney World. And to my book champions at Disney Hyperion, Tracey and Esther!

CONTENTS

CHAPTER 1

POPPING AWAY

 Gabby Gomez had finally popped the truth to her family: Gabby is the gumazing GUM GIRL!

Gabby's big secret was a happy surprise for her family—but the runaway Ferris wheel was a big disaster for the City Carnival!

With a chomp of sugar-free gum and the help of Ninja-Rina, Gabby had stretched to the rescue. The Ferris wheel smashed . . . and crashed . . . and bashed . . .

CRASH!

. . . but Gum Girl and Ninja-Rina proved that teamwork can overcome *any* challenge.

NOW . . . It was almost time for school break. Finally! Getting home from school, though, was anything *but* a break from Gabby's slightly-less-sticky, sugar-free superpowers. With the help of her **Sour Apple Blast** gum, she had to . . .

Stop a super-swoosh waterslide slipup!

Juggle a dim sum dumpling disaster!

That evening, Gabby was happy and tired.

"We are so proud of you," Mami said. "You told us the truth, and how you are using your powers to do so much good."

Gabby smiled.

Mrs. Gomez continued, "I think it's time you meet someone very special, someone who can teach you a lot."

"Really?" Gabby asked.

"¡Sí! We're going on a trip to visit my brother, your *tío*, in Cobá, México. I even got you travel-size peanut butter."

Before Gabby could ask questions, a loud crash sent her and Mrs. Gomez rushing to the living room.

Rico had constructed a massive obstacle course in the living room. And Dr. Gomez had arrived home just in time to see it.

"¡Mira, Papi!" Rico said proudly.

Rico turned to Gabby. "Can you time me?" He plopped a stopwatch into Gabby's hand and tied a towel around his neck as a cape.

Suddenly, Rico . . .

Catapulted over a tower!

Burrowed through a dark tunnel!

And bounded across a lava river!

Rico ran the course again, and again, and AGAIN . . . determined to do it faster each time.

"Bravo, Rico!" Gabby yelled. She gave Rico a high five as Dr. and Mrs. Gomez cheered.

Rico's smile was almost as wide as the lava river.

"Rico," Gabby said when he stopped to catch his breath. "If you could be a superhero, who would you be?"

"I would be your sidekick, Running Rico!"

He ran in place as fast as he could.

"No . . . no . . . I would be . . . the Super Stretcher!"

Rico thought a moment.

"No . . . wait . . . no . . . I would be . . . BUBBLE BOY!"

Rico climbed to the top of the couch, then jumped in the air, curling his body into a ball. "Exploding all over crime!"

Gabby giggled. "Well, I'm not too sure about that, Rico. It sounds a bit dangerous to me."

"No, I won't explode. I will . . . distract the criminals by blowing bubbles! Lots of bubbles everywhere! No one could stop . . . no one could . . . stop—"

Rico's voice began to fade and his excitement was replaced with a wide yawn.

Slowly, Gabby laid him down on the cozy couch cushions, then draped his cape over him as a snuggly blanket.

CHAPTER 2

HEART AND SOL

The last day before break, Ms. Smoot spoke to the class. "Remember that learning happens *everywhere*, not only in school!"

Gabby said good-bye to Ms. Smoot and her friends and bolted from school. Cobá, México, awaited!

As always, Gabby had a few last-minute things to do before she left for vacation. . . .

THE NEXT DAY . . . On the plane, Gabby and Rico watched the clouds roll by their window. They had never been to México—and they had never met their uncle because he was always

traveling around the world. Gabby took out a map and showed Cobá, México, to Rico.

"We're almost there!" she said.

"I can't wait!" said Rico.

The plane bumped to a landing. "*Mis niños*, we're here!" Mrs. Gomez called out. "*¡Vamos!*"

WHUP WHUP WHUP

The air felt warm and exciting as they got off the plane. They gathered their bags and waited for Gabby's *tío*. But where was he?

SUDDENLY . . . . A helicopter landed right in front of them.

A masked wrestler
jumped out!

DUN! DUN! DUN!

Mrs. Gomez ran toward the wrestler. Gabby put her hand in her pocket and grabbed her last piece of Sugar-Free Sour Apple Blast just in case her mom needed help.

But Mrs. Gomez had everything under control. She put the masked man in a headlock, squeezing tightly.

Mrs. Gomez laughed and then hugged the wrestler. She turned toward Gabby and Rico. "This is your *tío*, Sol Azteca!"

Gabby and Rico stared as Sol Azteca stepped toward them. He put his hand to his heart. "*In Lak'ech Ala K'in*," he said. That didn't sound like Spanish to Gabby and Rico. They furrowed their eyebrows and waited.

"It is a sacred Mayan greeting, *mis sobrinos*. It means 'I am you, and you are me.'"

Sol Azteca swept Rico and Gabby up into a big hug.

"I was sworn to secrecy, mija. *¿Verdad*, hermano?" Mrs. Gomez asked her brother.

"*¡Sí!*" Sol leaned toward Gabby. "And we have lots to talk about, Chica Chicle."

Gabby realized that her *tío* had a secret identity, just like she did. Luchadores always wear their masks to protect their identity. Gabby looked at her uncle with awe.

Rico, wide-eyed in disbelief, yelled, "I can't believe we're related to a masked luchador! And not just any wrestler, but **Sol Azteca!**" Rico continued.

"I've watched all of your matches!

My favorite was when you teamed up with the Evenhander against those tricky Rudos!

I loved your signature move off the top ropes!"

Sol Azteca smiled gratefully. *"Gracias*, Rico."
When Rico was finally finished, Sol turned to the rest of the family.

CHAPTER 3

TREE-MENDOUS POWER

Sol Azteca's helicopter rushed over the treetops of the Yucatán peninsula.

It swooped through wispy, whooshing clouds.

Finally, it hovered above a lush jungle. "The Maya had an advanced civilization," Sol explained over the headphones. "Much of it we are still unearthing."

The blades of the copter slowed as they descended into a tiny clearing. "Hold on tight!" said Sol.

Once the copter landed, Sol jumped out. "Welcome to the ancient ruins of Cobá, my home away from home."

Thick vines and trees hung heavy with fruit.
   A green quetzal soared overhead, his song calling
out to them. "That's Ikal," Sol pointed out. "This
was his home long before I arrived."

Hidden in the jungle nearby stood an ancient Maya pyramid.

"Whoa!" Rico said.

"That is the tallest pyramid in all the ancient ruins of Cobá," Gabby's *tío* said. "*¡Vamos!* I'll show you around."

INSIDE . . . Glass covered the walls where ancient artifacts lay. Plants grew everywhere. The stones of the pyramid hummed with life. And the beautiful quetzal circled high above them.

A soft breeze blew through the cracks of the pyramid walls. Right then, Gabby knew that this place was a part of her. She felt it deep in her soul and in her heart. The breeze turned into a strong, warm wind. To Gabby, it felt as though her ancestors were embracing and welcoming her.

The Gomez family continued to
follow Sol deeper into the pyramid.
In the far corner was a great wrestling ring.
Voices echoed off the pyramid walls
as four kids appeared.

"These are my students: Miguel, Alma, Lucas, and Litza," Sol said. "They are from my wrestling academy, Jaguares."

Rico stepped up to the ring, starstruck, as each student came forward and greeted the Gomez family. "*In Lak'ech Ala K'in.*"

Sol then called the team into a circle. They placed their hands together, then raised them in unison, yelling out, "KNOWLEDGE IS *FUERZA*!"

Sol smiled with pride and turned to Gabby's family. "I teach my students that wisdom is where true power lies, not muscle and tussle."

Miguel tugged on Sol's sleeve. "When will we get our masks, Maestro Sol? The Cocodrilos already have theirs!"

"*Paciencia*, my students," Sol said. "Remember what we've been learning? Masks are a rite of passage. They are earned after much hard work and dedication."

Rico jumped into the ring with the group of students.

"Who are the Cocodrilos?" Gabby asked her uncle.

"They are the students of my old wrestling partner, the Underhander."

"*Old* partner," Gabby said. "You're not partners anymore?"

"It's a long story, *sobrinita*. My old partner always wanted to win. And the more we won, the more he wanted to win."

"I don't understand," Gabby said. "If you were already winning, wasn't that enough?"

"For the Underhander? No. He hated to lose. We had a chance at the championship title—the highest honor in all México for a luchador.

But before the match began, the Evenhander greased the bottoms of our opponents' boots. And he put itching powder inside their masks."

"*¡Ai, no!* What did you do?" Gabby asked.

"I made a very big decision. Instead of facing the other team, I faced *him*."

"What?!" Gabby said. "You fought your own partner?"

"That's right. I had to stand up for what I believed in. Cheating is wrong. I wrestled him, and I won. He was shamed out of the ring."

Sol breathed in deeply. "That day, the Evenhander became the Underhander. He has vowed to show all México his true strength."

CHAPTER 4

JAG-UAR YOU READY?

"*Vamos.* Let me show you around," Sol called to his family. "This is my day job: collecting artifacts. I am an archaeologist. And I'm a wrestler by night!"

They passed a beautiful stone slab that had carvings of positions of the sun and moon. "This is a solar calendar," Sol said. "The Maya were great astronomers. They studied the skies and used the stars to help know when it was best to plant and harvest crops. They could even predict solar eclipses."

Sol pointed at two circles on the outer edge of the stone. "See how the light from the top of the temple streams, almost touching this area?"

Gabby and her family nodded.

"This tells us that we're due for a solar eclipse. It should happen tomorrow morning."

"Whoa!" Gabby and Rico said together.

Sol continued past huge stone statues, walls with hieroglyphs, and a collection of ancient vases. He stopped by a large Jade Jaguar. It was wedged high above, between two thick pillars near the center of the pyramid.

"If that **Jade Jaguar** is held during a solar eclipse, it releases the power of ten jaguars," Sol explained. "In English, the saying goes:

> *When day turns to night,*
> *Hold the Jade Jaguar tight.*
> *For the power of ten*
> *Will be with you then."*

Gabby tried to imagine the power of ten jaguars.

¡Diez jaguares!

They continued walking toward a sparkling pool of water. "What's this?" Gabby asked.

"Ah, *aquí tenemos un cenote*. It is the start of a waterway used thousands of years ago. See, look!" Sol led them past the sparkling pool to an aqueduct. "The water flows from the aqueduct to the Pool of Destiny."

Gabby's eyes widened. "The *what* . . . ?"

"The Pool of Destiny. It helps people discover their true selves—who they really are," Sol explained.

Gabby wondered what it meant to discover who you *really* are.

Mrs. Gomez came up beside them. "I'm so proud of you, Raúl. And I am so inspired."

"*You* have always inspired me, *hermanita*!" Sol said. "You taught me to pursue my biggest dreams, archaeology and wrestling. Even though most of the world would think that idea was crazy. Now I fight for what's right in the ring, and wrestle to save our ancient past."

Sol led them deeper into the pyramid. Everyone strolled around the space, looking at all the artifacts.

"Do you want to see something truly special?" Sol asked Gabby.

"*Sí, Tío!*"

Sol pointed to a tree at the back of the pyramid. "That, Gabriella, is a chicozapote tree. Have you heard of it?"

Gabby shook her head.

"The ancient Maya and Aztecs used something very special from this tree. Something called *tzicli*. It is chewy and sticky. It later came to be called *chicle*."

As Sol said the word *chicle*, the quetzal landed at the top of the tree and looked down at both of them.

"This tree is where part of your story begins, Gabriella."

Gabby walked over and put her hand on the trunk. She had always loved gum, and now she was touching the very place where gum came from: right here in México. Right where her family came from, too. Gabby was beginning to realize how deep the roots of her superpower were.

CHAPTER 5

CHEWS
YOUR
MOVES

The Gomez family was excited to stay at **Sol Azteca's** house.

Rico was busy climbing every tree around the yard. Inside, Gabby flipped through some of her uncle's library books. Her mind raced with everything she had learned that day.

"Time for bed now. We've got a big day of exploring tomorrow," Dr. Gomez called out to Gabby and Rico.

While Dr. and Mrs. Gomez tucked Rico in, Sol asked Gabby an important question: "Tomorrow, Chica Chicle, how about we train together?"

"¡Claro que sí!" she exclaimed.

"Okay, then! Tomorrow, we begin!"

THE NEXT DAY . . . Sol and Gabby arrived at the pyramid early. The Jade Jaguar sparkled in the light of the morning sun.

Gabby looked up toward it, but Sol caught her eye.

"Remember, knowledge is the most important part of strength," he said. "It's not *how* strong you are that matters, but *how* you choose to use that strength. *¿Entiendes?*"

Gabby nodded.

Suddenly, Sol tossed a ball at Gabby's feet!
"Wha—"

Gabby didn't have time to think. Sol tossed another ball to her right. Then to her left.

"Don't focus on strength, Gabriella, focus on *knowledge*, remember? You can't stop these balls with strength alone. Use your head and your heart, too!" Sol yelled with a smile.

Gabby thought quickly, then noticed the pattern. *Right, left, left, right*. Once she discovered the pattern, Gabby quickly moved from side to side to dodge the balls!

"*¡Excelente*, Gabriella!" Sol said. "You did it! You used your mind to figure out the solution. And you did it *without* your superpower!"

Just then, the quetzal flew into the pyramid.

"Now let's practice with some gummy power."

Sol held out a few pieces of gum. "Your mom told me it had to be sugar-free, so I found the finest flavors in all of México. You choose: Papaya Power, Guava Greatness, or Mango Mystery."

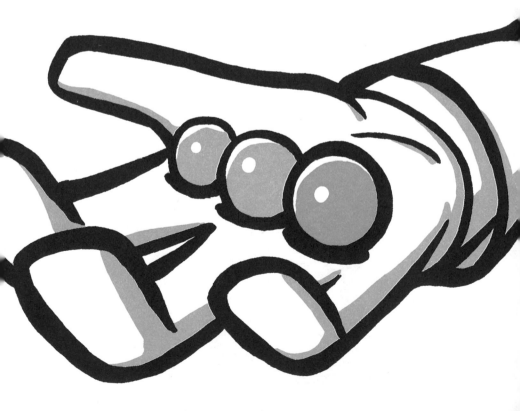

Gabby looked at the flavors and imagined herself as each one. . . .

She reached for the Papaya Power. Suddenly, the quetzal swooped close to her hand. It sang out as it swished toward the peak of the pyramid.

Gabby thought for a moment. *Knowledge is the real strength.* She took a breath and picked the Mango Mystery gumball.

"*¡Muy bien, sobrinita!*" Sol exclaimed. "You have chosen wisely. Now, let's see just how to use your superpowers even when they're a bit less sticky."

Gabby reached into her pocket and pulled out her last piece of Sugar-Free Sour Apple Blast. "Wait, Tío! Let's trade first!"

"*¡Gracias!*" Sol took Gabby's gift.

Sol chewed. "Whoa!"

Sol puckered. "This IS sour!"

Sol blew . . . the gum right out!

"This is too sour for me!" he laughed, and picked up the gum. "Ready to try Mango Mystery now?"

"*¡Lista!*" Gabby said. She popped the gumball into her mouth.

"So . . . *orange!*"

"Amazing!" Sol clapped as Gum Girl burst to life. "Let's go, Chica Chicle!"

Sol showed Gabby how to take advantage of her less-sticky, sugar-free power by . . .

Thinking faster!

Reaching farther!

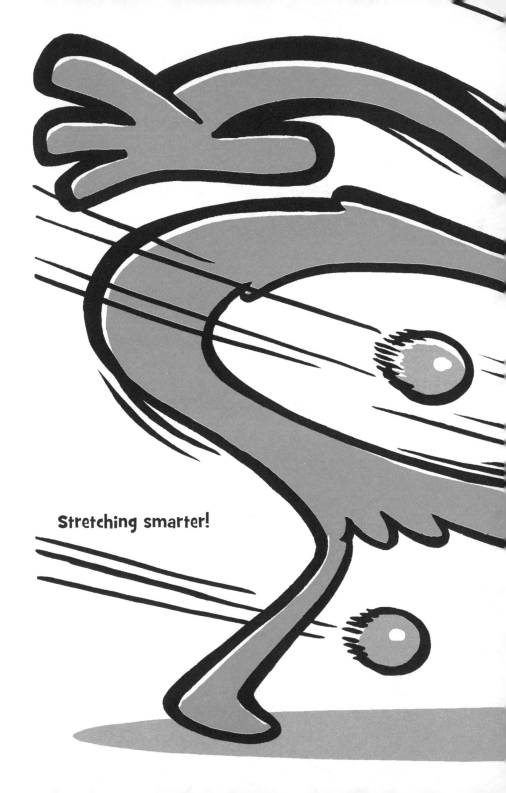

Stretching smarter!

"*Muy bien*, Chica Chicle!" Sol threw multiple balls all at once. "Use your surroundings!"

Gum Girl reached for a large stone.

Then she blocked all the balls in one move. "Great work!" Sol clapped in amazement.

"This superpower is a gift. You must use your power to help the helpless. You are the hope in the *lucha* of life."

"Now, what do you say we tell your parents and Rico all about how—"

SUDDENLY . . . A group of mysterious luchadores stomped into the camp.

"Sol Azteca, I challenge you and your school to a match! I'll show you who is the strongest!"

CHAPTER 6

SWEET REVENGE

"It's payback time, **Sol!**" The Underhander raised his fist and smashed it into his other hand. "You robbed me of my win!"

To protect her identity, Gum Girl ducked behind a wall and quickly turned back to Gabby.

Sol turned to the Underhander. "Old friend, let's talk this through. I'm sure——"

"The time for talking is over, Sol! *You* were the one who stole the championship belt from me. I lost because of **YOU. I** could have been the best!"

Sol's students approached to see what the commotion was all about.

"Being the best by cheating means nothing at all." Sol Azteca moved in front of the Jade Jaguar, as he noticed the Underhander becoming mesmerized by it.

"Enough talking, Sol! Action is more powerful than words! Cocodrilos, to the ring! Let's show the Jaguares what real wrestling looks like! Now, I will prove to all México that I am the true champion," the Underhander roared.

The students gathered across from one another, squaring up for the wrestling match.

"We want a fair, safe match," Sol Azteca said, looking at his wrestlers and the Underhander's. "¡Sí!" his own students shouted back. The Underhander pushed his way in. "Less talking, more wrestling! Let's go!"

The Underhander raised his hand in the air, and his students approached.

Gabby met across from her opponent in the center of the pyramid. They would wrestle first while the other students waited to be tagged in for their turns.

From behind the mask her opponent wore, loud laughter rumbled.

"Huh? How do you know me?!" Gabby asked.

"HA-HA! A luchador never tells her true identity!" the masked opponent replied.

Gabby racked her brain trying to place the voice.

NO!

IT COULDN'T BE!

"NATALIE GOOCH?!"

"What are you doing here, Natalie?"

"I used my Gum Girl T-shirt money to go to wrestling camp. What are YOU doing here?"

Gabby stumbled backward when she heard Natalie mention GUM GIRL.

"I—I—"

"Enough talking already!" The Underhander interrupted. "Time to wrestle!"

Natalie tested her newest move—the Dynamo Elbow—on Gabby.

Luckily, Gabby sidestepped Natalie's advance.

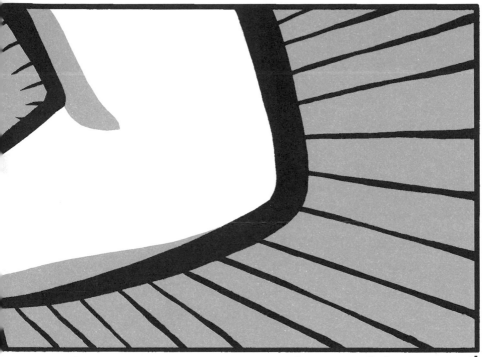

Unluckily, Natalie power-elbowed the wall of the pyramid!

The wall cracked.

KRACK!

"Yes! Again!" The Underhander roared out from his side of the ring.

"Nice, Gabriella!" called Sol. "Keep using your head!"

Natalie and Gabby continued their match. The other students cheered them on and held out their hands to be tagged in.

MEANWHILE . . . The Underhander slowly crept closer and closer to the Jade Jaguar. He continued to yell out, "Win by any means, Cocodrilos!"

Sol Azteca shook his head. "Use your heads! Be wise. Be smart."

Through the opening in the top of the pyramid, the bright morning sun began to darken a little.

What was going on?

Everyone looked up to see the moon moving over the sun, darkening the edges of the sun's bright power. Just then, Sol Azteca figured out that the Underhander was not here for the competition.

Inside the pyramid, it started to feel like night even though it was morning. Gabby suddenly remembered the solar calendar. The solar eclipse was about to happen!

CHAPTER 7

TANGO WITH MANGO

While the match tumbled on with students tagging one another in and out, the Underhander had double-axe-handled his way up the giant pillar to the Jade Jaguar.

Just as the sun started to disappear, the Underhander grabbed the Jade Jaguar.

DUN! DUN! DUN!

The pyramid began to

SHAKE!

and

RUMBLE!

and

CRRRUMBLE!

Giant stone chunks crashed down around the wrestlers. A piece fell right between Natalie and Gabby.

Realizing what had happened, Gabby yelled out to her uncle.

Sol hurried to stop the Underhander from escaping. Gabby watched and remembered what Sol had told her:

When day turns to night,
Hold the Jade Jaguar tight.
For the power of ten
Will be with you then.

She looked up: The moon was almost completely covering the sun! It was going to be a total solar eclipse.

The Underhander tried to push Sol Azteca out of his way. Sol used a double-leg down-block to stop him. The Underhander quickly threw dirt in Sol's face.

"You never learn, do you, Sol? I always win, and now I've won the most powerful prize of all!" The Underhander laughed and ran for the exit.

Gabby had to think *and* act—fast!

She reached into her pocket and pulled out a piece of Mango Mystery gum.

BOING!

Gum Girl turned into a wrestling ring!
Natalie Gooch stood to the side, shocked.

Gum Girl pulled the Underhander and Sol inside the ropes. The Underhander tested the strength of the ring. The dirt still stung in Sol's eyes. He struggled to see what was happening.

Gum Girl wondered if her move was enough to help. Or would the Underhander actually win?

CHAPTER 8

TAG-TEAM
DREAM

Sol, still partly blinded, stumbled through his wrestling moves. The Underhander took the upper hand. Just as all hope seemed to vanish, another hand reached into the ring.

"Tag me, Sol!"

Sol reached out and tagged the hand, stepping aside to recover his vision.

It couldn't be, Gum Girl thought, but she knew that voice TOO well.

The Jade Jaguar dropped to the ground just outside the gummy ring. The Jaguares thought fast, picked it up, and ran away.

Gum Girl popped back into shape as chunks of the pyramid kept falling.

Gum Girl felt a *plop* on her head. She looked up. It was Ikal, the quetzal, pecking at the chicozapote tree above her—and dropping chicle on Gum Girl's head.

That's it! Gum Girl thought. She could use the sap from the gum tree to stick the pyramid back together!

PLOP!

In an instant, Gum Girl was stuck on the chicozapote tree. She began scooping up the sap to put the pieces of the pyramid back together.

But . . .

The chicle was sticking to Gum Girl!

It stretched.

It pulled.

It glued!

This was a seriously super-sticky situation! *Too* sticky for Gum Girl . . . but maybe not for Gabby Gomez.

Gum Girl pulled out her handy
travel-size jar of peanut butter.
In a flash, Gabby Gomez was back!

Gabby ran here and there, and there and back here.
Another chunk of stone fell from the roof. It
crashed on top of the solar calendar.
What could be done?!

As Gabby stuffed more sap into the crumbling cracks of the pyramid, Natalie Gooch watched. Her head darted back and forth between the Underhander and Gabby.

Natalie thought she should help her teacher.
Then she thought she should help her classmate.
Gabby ran right, left, left, right, dodging falling
rocks and sticking them back in place.

HELP!

Natalie squinted her eyes, thinking:

Natalie scratched her head. *Gabby, gum,* she thought again. And then it hit her.

CHAPTER 9

TOWER OF POWER

Natalie remembered the rhino rescue, and the Ferris wheel fiasco, and *all* the times she had bullied Gabby Gomez.

All that time, Gabby was Gum Girl. She could have used her superpowers to easily stop Natalie Gooch. But she hadn't. Instead, she had used her powers for good.

Natalie had a decision to make.

And it was no longer a hard one.

"Gabby! Get on my shoulders!" Natalie called out.

Gabby climbed on top of Natalie's shoulders, reaching much higher than she could alone.

On the other side of the pyramid, the Underhander caught up to Sol's students. He snatched the Jade Jaguar away from them, but they pulled it back. Angry, the Underhander pulled it back even harder. But, just as the moon fully eclipsed the sun, the Jaguares wrestled the Jade Jaguar from the Underhander's grip.

The Underhander rose up in fierce anger. He lunged at the students. Suddenly, bubbles started popping above his head.

Confused, he looked up.

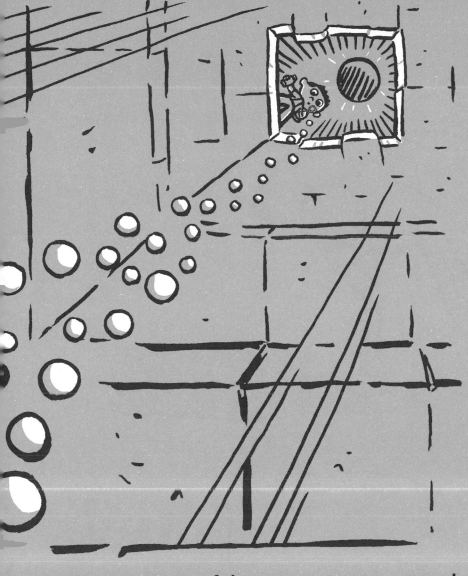

Rico was on top of the pyramid blowing bubbles!

The Underhander moved to get out of the way. He swayed left . . . then right . . . then back to the left. He couldn't hold on to his balance any longer.

He fell into the Pool of Destiny!

Everyone gathered around the water.

Rising up out of the pool moments later, the Underhander's face seemed calm. His eyes had a new light in them.

"Sol . . . I—I—"

"I know, my friend," Sol Azteca finished.

"Can you forgive me? I let winning ruin what I truly needed—a friend."

"Of course," Sol said, hugging his partner. "But as an old friend of mine likes to say, now is not the time for talking!" The pyramid was still crumbling around them. "We need to act, and fast!"

Gabby and Natalie raced up beside Sol Azteca and the Underhander. "We need to work together," Gabby said. "All of us!"

"You're right!" the Underhander agreed. "Cocodrilos," he yelled. "Hurry! Let's help!"

Gabby and Natalie had been trying to stick the pyramid together with the sap as fast as they could—but they couldn't do it alone.

Everyone started gluing the cracks back together with chicle.

Dr. Gomez led the way. He knew all about fillings!

Rico raced sap back and forth from the tree, collecting more chicle.

The great pillars started to shake and fall.

"It's not enough. We need the Jade Jaguar!" Gabby called out.

Natalie ran to the center of the pyramid. With all her might, she hopped up one of the stone pillars. Gabby climbed on Natalie's shoulders. But, to reach the top and replace the Jade Jaguar, they needed to be taller. Much taller.

Gabby reached for a Mango Mystery gumball. "¡Ai, no!"

She was out of gum!

Sol thought fast. "Students, TOWER OF POWER, go!"

The wrestlers began to build a ladder out of themselves. The Cocodrilos joined them. But they were *still* a little bit short.

"I'm coming!" Rico roared.

Rico climbed the tower of students with the Jade Jaguar in his hand. He slammed the stone back into place.

THUNK

The pyramid was saved!
Natalie and Gabby looked at each other with relief.

CHAPTER 10

THE LUCHADOR IN YOU!

As the sun streaked the morning sky, the *Cocodrilos* and the *Jaguares* faced one another in two lines, just as they had the day before. This time, instead of fighting, each student stepped forward to stand beside the other.

"This is a very special day," Sol began. "When you uncover your true power, you earn your mask."

Sol looked at his old partner. The Evenhander spoke: "We *all* need to remember our true power."

"From now on, we are no longer two schools. We are together. *JUNTOS!*" Sol said. "We coach together. We wrestle together."

Sol continued: "In recognition of the difficult task you have worked together to accomplish, it is our great honor to present you with new masks.

Please step forward Kid Jaguar, Lightning Lobo, Narwhal Niña, and Pink Puma!" Miguel, Alma, Lucas, and Litza were beaming.

Then, Sol added, "And we have a special honor today. Rico Gomez, please come forward."

As Rico approached, Sol gave him a wrestling outfit. "This was my first uniform. I now give it to someone with heart, hope, and smarts."

AT THE AIRPORT . . .

"It's going to feel a little dull without you all here," Sol Azteca said.

"Oh, I'm sure you've got a few new adventures up your sleeve, *hermanito*," Mrs. Gomez said. "What's next for you?"

Sol thought for a while. "Well, there is another archaeological site we're going to excavate next week."

"Wow, another site already?" Mrs. Gomez asked.

"What can I say, I dig it!" Sol responded.

Dr. and Mrs. Gomez laughed.

But Sol noticed that his niece was not laughing. He bent down beside her, just as the family had reached the baggage checkpoint.

"*¿Qué pasa*, Gabriella?"

Gabby wiped away a tear and then looked at her uncle. "It's just that—well, I'm going to miss you, and this place."

"You are part of this place, Gabriella. And whether you knew it or not, it is part of you. It always has been."

"I'm going to miss all of you," Sol said.

"Don't worry, Tío," Rico said. "Bubble Boy and Gum Girl will be back again, because . . . because . . ."

"This is our home, too," Gabby finished.

Sol smiled.

Gabby and Rico gave Tío a massive hug.

Sol hugged them back with all his heart. "*In Lak'ech Ala K'in. I am you, you are me.*"

"*In Lak'ech Ala K'in,*" Gabby and Rico said together.

Gabby knew she was a part of something much bigger than just herself. *We all are,* she thought.

SALAS 7-9 ⬆

JUST THEN . . .

Natalie Gooch walked up
to the airport gate. She
was all alone.

Gabby saw Natalie differently after they had teamed up together. Something that had seemed impossible before now felt possible after watching the Underhander become the Evenhander.

Gabby ran over to meet her. "Hey, Natalie. Do you, uh, want to sit with us?"

Natalie's face showed surprise and nervousness, then quickly turned to relief.

"Sure," Natalie replied.

Together, they walked back toward the Gomez family. "Everyone, this is my friend Natalie."

BACK AT SCHOOL . . .

Ms. Smoot was nowhere to be found when Gabby and Natalie returned to their class. Their substitute teacher was there instead. But he was acting VERY strange. . . .

DUN! DUN! DUN!

Children's 510
[redacted]
Cover blown !
[redacted] Gum Girl !,